11-3049

The Promise and Perils of Technology™

PRIVACY,
DATA HARVESTING,
AND YOU

Jeri Freedman

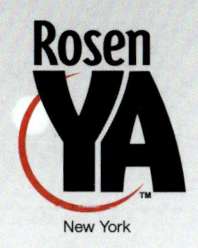

Rosen YA
New York

Published in 2020 by The Rosen Publishing Group, Inc.
29 East 21st Street, New York, NY 10010

Copyright © 2020 by The Rosen Publishing Group, Inc.

First Edition

All rights reserved. No part of this book may be reproduced in any form without permission in writing from the publisher, except by a reviewer.

Library of Congress Cataloging-in-Publication Data

Names: Freedman, Jeri, author.
Title: Privacy, data harvesting, and you / Jeri Freedman.
Description: First edition. | New York: Rosen Publishing, 2020. | Series: The promise and perils of technology | Includes bibliographical references and index. | Audience: Grades 7 to 12.
Identifiers: LCCN 2018046288 | ISBN 9781508188315 (library bound) | ISBN 9781508188308 (pbk.)
Subjects: LCSH: Data mining—Juvenile literature. | Internet—Safety measures—Juvenile literature. | Privacy, Right of—Juvenile literature.
Classification: LCC QA76.9.D343 F7347 2020 | DDC 006.3/12—dc23
LC record available at https://lccn.loc.gov/2018046288

Manufactured in the United States of America

CONTENTS

	Introduction	4
1	Harvesting Data	7
2	The Right to Privacy	16
3	Online Consumer Nation	24
4	The Power of Persuasion	32
5	Protecting Your Data	41
	Glossary	48
	For More Information	51
	For Further Reading	54
	Bibliography	56
	Index	61

INTRODUCTION

Data harvesting, or web scraping, is a process in which a small script, often called a bot, is used to automatically extract large amounts of data from websites and use this data for purposes other than those for which it was intended. Bots can be used to collect information on people for a variety of reasons, both benign and malignant. It can be used without permission to capture website information, such as text, photos, email addresses, and contact lists. Data harvesting is closely tied to data mining, the process of analyzing large amounts of data collected from company databases. One of the key issues raised by data harvesting and data mining technology is that of individual privacy. Data harvesting and mining allow companies and other organizations to capture and analyze business and financial transactions and, in the process, to glean a significant amount of data about individuals' buying habits and preferences. This data can be used to deduce a person's demographic characteristics, such as age, gender, health, ethnicity, socioeconomic status, and sexual orientation. Thus, it reveals facts that an individual might prefer to keep private. This information can be used for positive or negative purposes.

In 2016, the Edelman public relations firm and the University of Cambridge Psychometrics Research Centre conducted a survey of people's attitudes toward data mining, machine learning, and

Introduction

When teens buy items online, websites capture a variety of data about their preferences and characteristics.

related technologies used by companies to collect and analyze people's personal data. The survey, *Trust and Predictive Technologies 2016*, included more than thirty-four thousand people worldwide. The results revealed that 71 percent of people believed that companies that had access to their personal data were using it unethically. Only 26 percent trusted the government not to sell their data. There was support for using data for purposes that would improve health and welfare, but much less support for its commercial use. Eighty-four percent of people supported the use of data mining to improve health care. However, merely 47 percent believed it should be used to set the price of car insurance. Similarly, they were in favor of the use of such technologies to help them manage their finances, but not to decide automatically who should get a mortgage or loan. These attitudes represent a realistic assessment of many of the applications and dangers of data mining that will be discussed in this resource.

The material here explains what data harvesting and data mining are and how they are carried out. The importance of privacy is covered. Two of the most common applications of data harvesting and data mining are discussed: selling products and services and influencing people's attitudes toward political issues. Because of the potential to misuse people's data, there is a great deal of support for some type of governmental regulation and enforcement to protect people's privacy. In the United States, however, it is unlikely that there will be regulation of the collection and use of people's data any time soon. One reason for this is that, as of 2018, the country has a president and Congress that are exceedingly probusiness and antiregulation. A series of actions that individuals can take to help protect their data and their privacy will be provided here.

CHAPTER 1

Harvesting Data

Data harvesting is a means of collecting data from websites on the internet. Data mining is the process of analyzing large amounts of collected data. People face issues from both these activities.

Data Harvesting

Data harvesting, also called web scraping, uses pieces of computer code called scripts to capture users' personal information. These scripts automatically search through the data that organizations collect through their websites. The scripts are often referred to as bots. Data harvesting takes place on the computers of companies and organizations, not on individuals' computers. A script is designed to search through the information on an organization's servers and extract user data. Once the information is collected, it can be used for an array of purposes. Such uses range from targeting users for advertising to stealing Social Security numbers to commit identity theft. Some bots are able to access every record in a company's database to obtain information. Because creating bots is cheap and easy, it's simple for hackers to implement. They can access user data on websites without permission to steal not only textual data, but also photos and email addresses. Illicitly obtained email addresses can be used to send targeted emails to the website's users.

Not all data is harvested illegally. Sometimes organizations use bots to harvest large amounts of data about their own customers.

Privacy, Data Harvesting, and You

This photograph of a data center with streaming data illustrates the millions of pieces of data that are collected and analyzed every day.

They then sell the data to third parties (often called partners) that use it to promote products or for research. This practice is legal, but is it an acceptable policy? Facebook provided users' data to a British political consulting firm called Cambridge Analytica. Cambridge Analytica later misused the data, causing Facebook to alter its policies. The gay, bisexual, and transgender dating website

Harvesting Data

Grindr harvests data from its users. The data it collects includes the phone ID, email address, global positioning system (GPS) location, and, most significantly, HIV status for each user. In a shocking breach of trust, Grindr gave third-party companies Appitimize and Localytics access to this data. The data shared included users' HIV status—which is generally considered confidential medical information. Grindr claims the data was not sold but shared to help in optimizing the app, but users were outraged at this violation of their privacy. As a result, Grindr no longer collects HIV status information. It still shares other information about its users.

Data harvesting is lucrative. Private companies, called data aggregators, harvest data from a range of websites for use by clients who pay them a fee. Data aggregation companies are legal. However, their collection and use of people's data is controversial. One example is BrightPlanet. This company performs data harvesting using bots they have created. It stores the data on computer servers it owns and provides access to the database for its clients through an application called a portal dashboard. This portal dashboard allows clients to obtain data that matches specific criteria. The questionable nature of this activity is emphasized by the fact that BrightPlanet's website states: "It is best to harvest from generally anonymous reverse IP address servers which are not easily attributable back to BrightPlanet or the client." (The internet protocol [IP] address is a unique number that allows a computer on the internet to be identified and contacted.) BrightPlanet also uses a technology that rotates, or alternates, the IP addresses used to contact the company's servers to avoid detection as

Privacy, Data Harvesting, and You

Facebook chief executive officer Mark Zuckerberg testifies before a US congressional committee in the wake of the Cambridge Analytica scandal.

an entity performing data harvesting. The fact that the organization doesn't want to be identified as the entity searching for information emphasizes the dubiousness of this activity. Organizations such as this can collect data from companies, news providers, classified listings, social media, patent databases, security auditing logs, proprietary company information, and even job boards, among other sources.

Legal data aggregators themselves can be the target of illegal data aggregators. In 2013, it was revealed that a number of legal data aggregators, including LexisNexis, Dun & Bradstreet, and Kroll Background America, had been hacked by the illegal data harvesting organization SSNDOB. In turn, a group of teenage white-hat hackers, who call themselves hacktivists, hacked SSNDOB and revealed that a vast amount of data had been collected by SSNDOB, including sensitive information, such as Social Security and credit

Harvesting and Data Mining Health Care Data

Data mining medical information is of great interest to hospitals, the government, and insurance companies, which want to improve outcomes and reduce costs. Medical data is located in patients' electronic records, which are kept in databases on computer systems. So, before medical data can be analyzed, it must be extracted from sources such as hospitals, health care organizations, government Medicare records, and the like. Data can be extracted by text processing and sorting coded medical records. The data is then data mined. Individual patient profiles can be created, or patients with similar profiles can be grouped. This vast amount of data is called big data. Big medical data can contribute to medical research by providing information to decision support systems. (A decision support system consists of computers, programs, and data that help an organization with analysis and decision making.) These systems compile data on particular symptoms. Doctors and researchers use the information to identify patient problems and to find patterns in the progression of certain diseases and patients' responses to treatment. Medical data is also used to detect patterns that might indicate Medicare or insurance fraud. Under these circumstances, a big challenge is keeping patients' medical data secure. Data harvesting and hacking have resulted in data breaches. According to an article in *Forbes* magazine, "In 2014, medical records accounted for 43 percent of all data stolen" in the health care sector. In addition to the theft and possible exposure of patients' medical data, many people object to their personal medical data being used for purposes such as research without their approval or knowledge.

Privacy, Data Harvesting, and You

card numbers, which SSNDOB sold for purposes such as identity theft. Victims even included celebrities, such as Beyoncé.

Companies have means to ensure that queries from customers are coming from a human being, not from a bot trying to gain access to the system. One such method is the captcha, the Completely Automated Public Turing test to tell Computers and Humans Apart. The captcha is an image containing a variety of letters and numbers. It is displayed below a form that the user fills out online. The user is requested to type the letters and numbers and often to check a

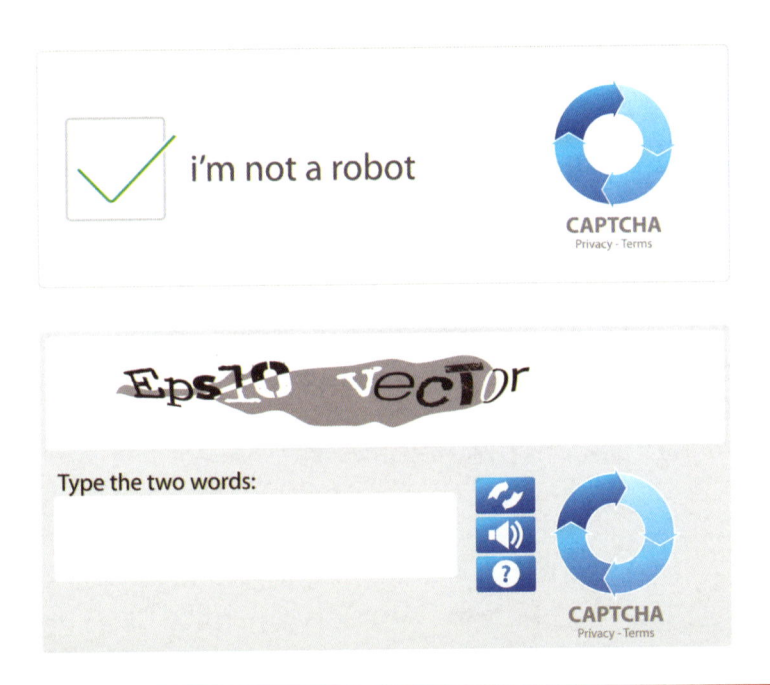

This example of a captcha shows an arrangement of letters that can be read by a human being but not a computer.

box that says, "I am not a robot," or something similar. Because the captcha is an image and not text, the script cannot read it, but a human being can.

Data Mining

In contrast to data harvesting, data mining is the use of software by companies to analyze large quantities of data collected by companies about their customers in the course of conducting business and kept in their databases. Such vast quantities of data collected by companies and organizations are called big data, and the large databases that store harvested data are called data warehouses. The goal of data mining is to discover patterns in the data. For example, Amazon analyzes customer purchases to find out which products customers might be likely to purchase in the future, on the basis of past purchases. Big data is too large to be analyzed by human beings. Instead, companies use computer programs called algorithms to search through the data. Algorithms consist of a set of rules that can be applied to searched data. Some companies sell their accumulated customer data and analysis to other companies, which allows them to target the customers for retail or other purposes. In contrast to big data mining, which relies on data already collected, fast data mining searches for and identifies patterns in data while users are interacting with a website. The goal of fast data mining is to act on the data while the user is still engaged with the system. For example, if you download a song, a box might pop up suggesting similar products you might want to purchase.

Data mining becomes a particularly serious privacy issue when financial data and transactions are involved and when companies sell data to third parties. In addition, data mining has the ability to find information that a person might not even know, or might not want others to know. Articles in *Forbes* magazine and the *New York Times Magazine* recount an incident in which retailer Target identified that a teen was pregnant—before her father found out.

Privacy, Data Harvesting, and You

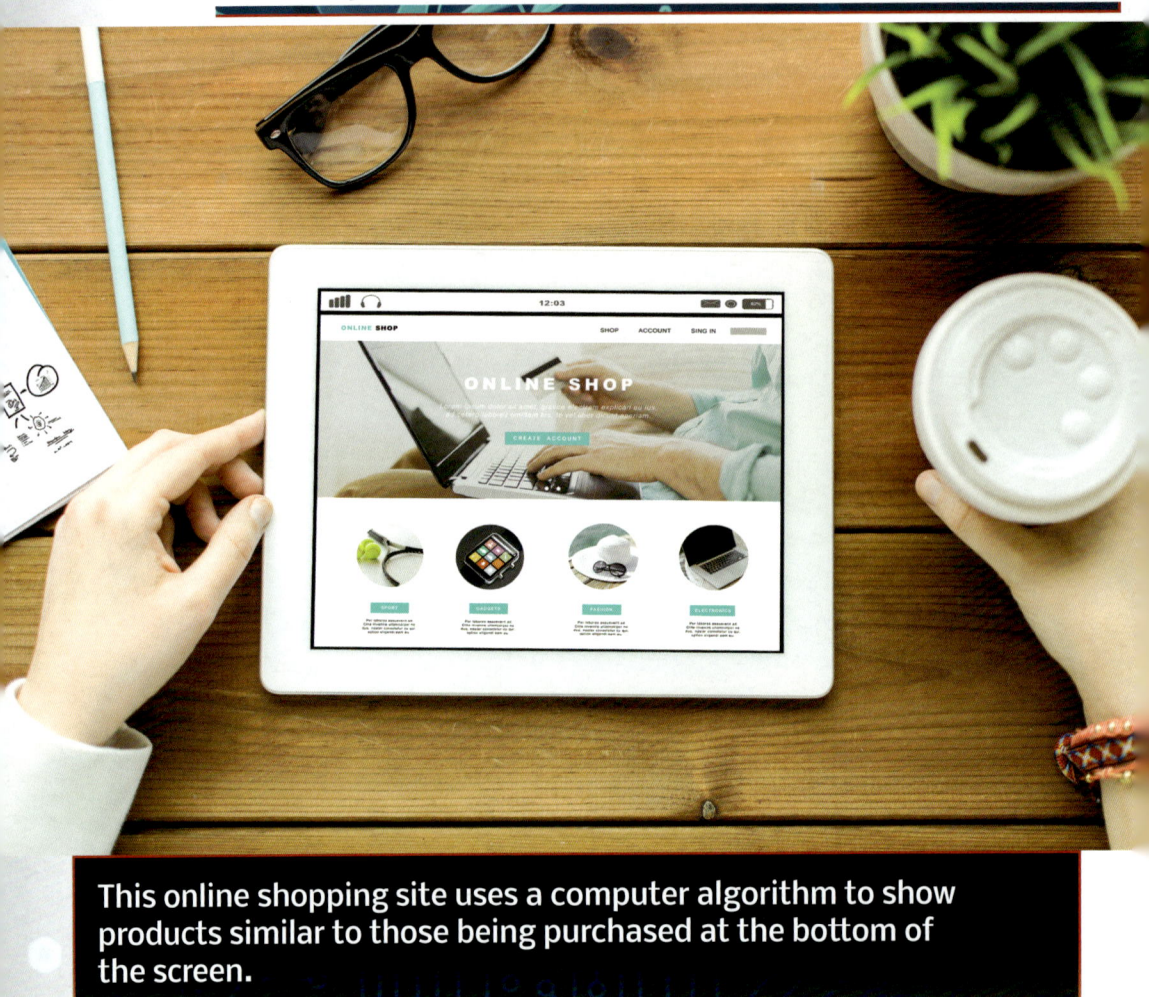

This online shopping site uses a computer algorithm to show products similar to those being purchased at the bottom of the screen.

Target routinely tries to identify women who might be pregnant. It can then secure them as customers for personal pregnancy and baby products. As reported by Kashmir Hill of *Forbes*, according to Target statistician Andrew Pole, Target assigns all of its customers a unique Guest ID number. Target attaches a record of everything the customer buys to this ID number. Computer algorithms then crawl through the data and analyze the customer's purchases. Target has identified approximately two dozen products that can be used to create a "pregnancy prediction" score. Even creepier—the company

14

can assign a likely due date for the baby's arrival! Target can then send coupons timed to very specific stages of a woman's pregnancy. According to Charles Duhigg in the *New York Times Magazine* article, one day a man stormed into a Minnesota Target store, waving a flyer advertising maternity clothes and cribs. He accused the manager of sending his high-school-aged daughter coupons encouraging her to get pregnant. The manager calmed the man down and called him a few days later to further apologize. Instead, the man apologized to the manager, stating he had spoken to his daughter, and she was indeed pregnant. In an understatement, in the article, Pole says, "If we send someone a catalog and say, 'Congratulations on your first child!' and they've never told us they're pregnant, that's going to make some people uncomfortable."

CHAPTER 2

The Right to Privacy

There is great controversy over the collection, use, and sale of data by companies and other organizations. Neither the Constitution nor the Bill of Rights guarantees citizens a right to privacy. However, many people feel strongly that their data is like their physical property. People feel it belongs to them, and they should decide when, how, and by whom it is used. Companies, on the other hand, especially those that provide services to users for free, claim that collecting data is necessary. It allows them to sell advertising, which makes it possible to provide those services for free, and to better target customers to sell more products and services.

Who Cares about Privacy Anyway?

Students today have grown up in a digital world, in which they often share every aspect of their lives with their friends, family, and sometimes complete strangers, via social media applications like Instagram, Snapchat, Facebook, and Twitter. According to a 2018 article by the Pew Research Center, "YouTube, Instagram and Snapchat are the most popular online platforms among teens. Fully 95 percent of teens have access to a smartphone, and 45 percent say they are online 'almost constantly.'"

Social media do allow people to maintain close connections to others who are important in their lives. It also helps them to provide support to friends and family on an immediate and a continuous

The Right to Privacy

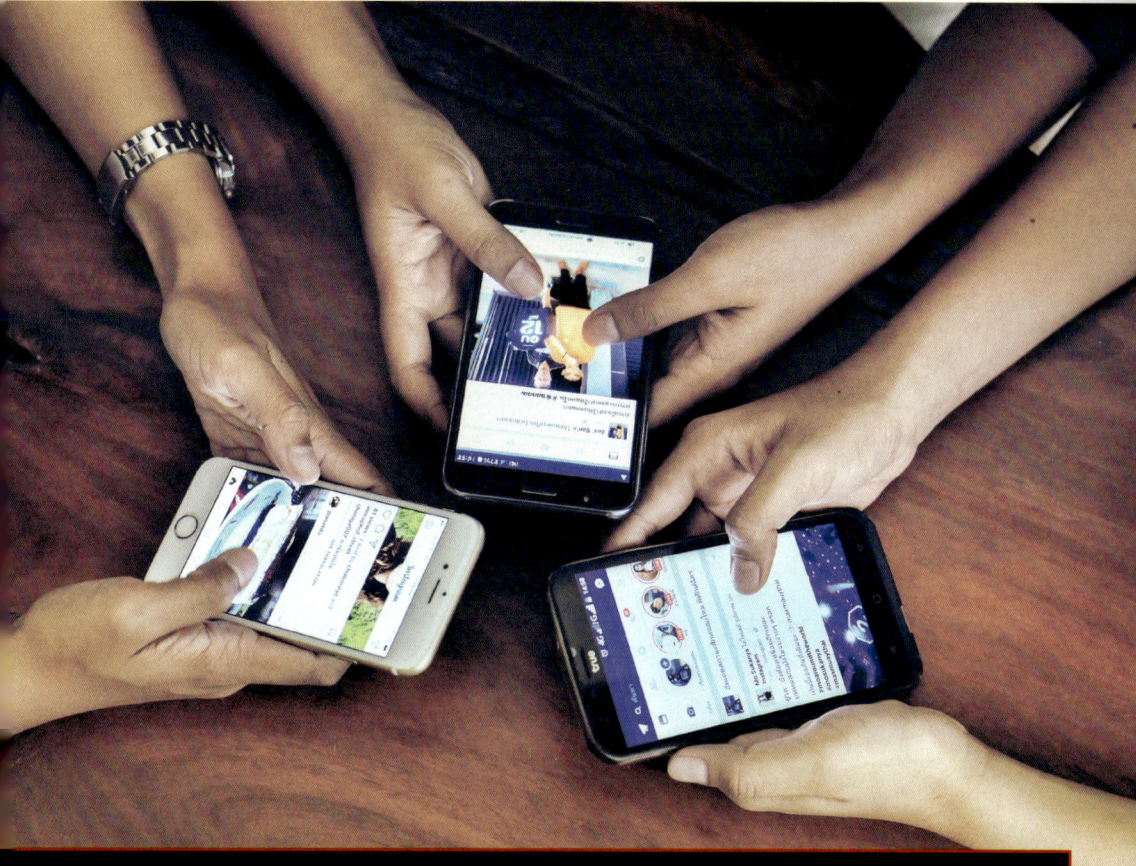

The constant use of social media by many teens can reduce the amount of time they spend in face-to-face interactions.

basis. Social media also make it easy to find out about the latest news and respond to it. The downside is that not all sources of news are reliable. There are other negative aspects to social media as well. They reduce the emphasis on face-to-face interactions. In addition, they can create a false impression of how people live because they can post just the exciting and successful things they do. This situation can lead teens to form a negative view of themselves because they feel they don't stack up to these distorted impressions. Social media can also be used to spread rumors or bully people who are different

Privacy, Data Harvesting, and You

or simply unpopular. Social media can create the false impression that everyone is sharing everything with everyone. This notion is not true. People edit what they share online, to make themselves look good. There are many aspects of people's lives they do not share with the world. So, is privacy important, and if so, why?

Teens are an important target market for advertisers and retailers. They often have money to spend and few expenses. Therefore, companies are motivated to collect data about them and use that data to sell them products. Some of these products, such as shoes, are benign, if sometimes expensive. However, other products, such as credit cards, can entrap people in debt that affects their lives for years. The fact is that privacy allows people to share what they want about themselves and not have a third party use or share that information. It enables people to do things that are legal, but that they may not want the whole world to know about. This concept is known as anonymity. For instance, people might support a political or social cause but not want to attract the attention of people who disagree with them. People might simply want to avoid being inundated with advertising for products or solicitations for money. They might not want everyone in the world, including potential employers and insurers, to know that they have a disease (such as hepatitis or AIDS), a disability, or a family history of a particular ailment. For example, the fact that one has a certain disease might negatively affect one's chances of being hired for a job. Companies are less inclined to hire people who will make medical claims and raise their insurance costs—or just take time off from work because of illness. Someone might not want to reveal his or her religion or sexual orientation. Even such apparently benign information as the fact that one travels extensively can have a negative impact. It could lead criminals to target one's home because it is likely to be empty. For these reasons, it is important that people have control over what information they reveal, when, and through what venues. Such control makes people safer, and feeling safer reduces their stress as well. Many people believe that it should be up to individuals to decide whether or not

The Right to Privacy

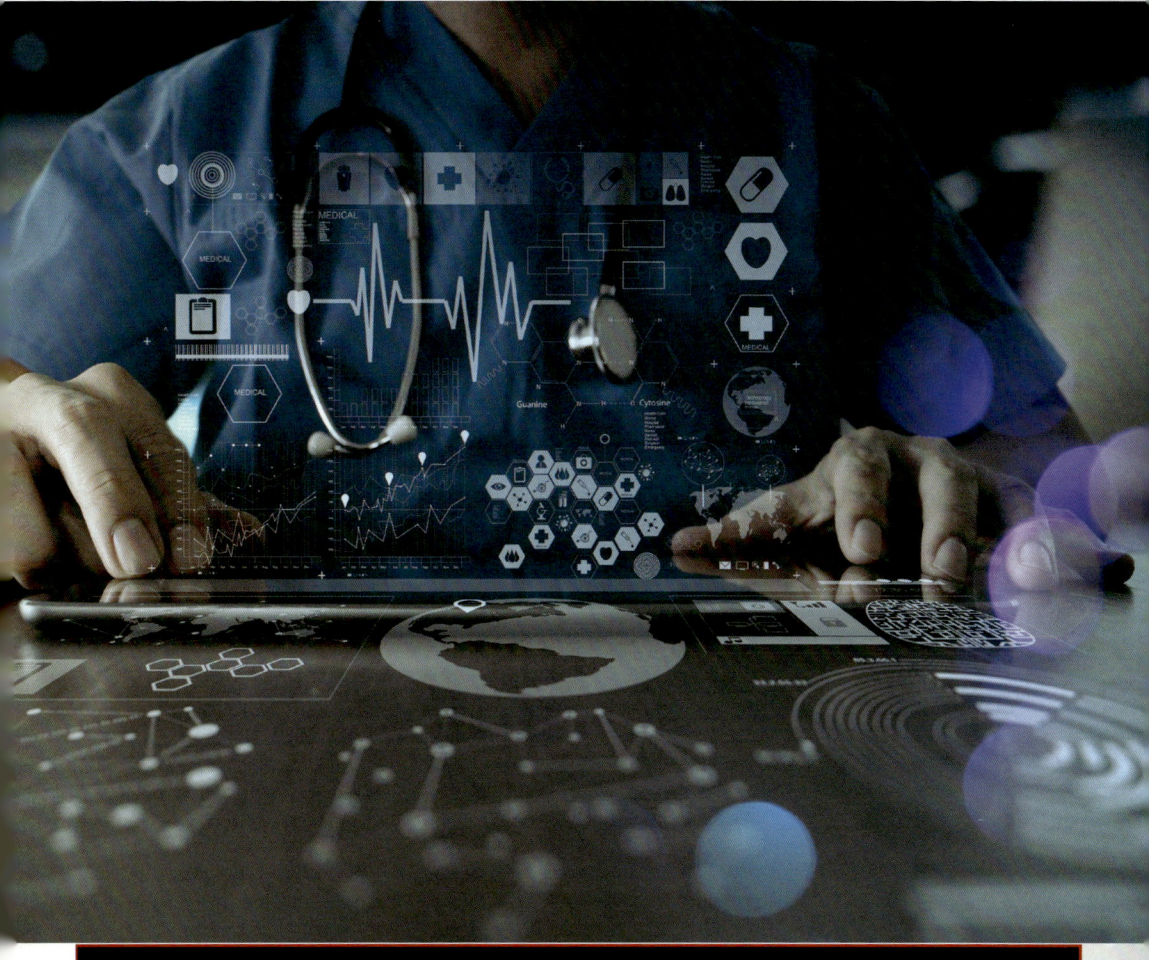

The capturing and analyzing of patients' data on computer systems for research raises concerns about confidential information being released or misused.

to share personal information. They believe that companies and organizations shouldn't be allowed to collect and distribute people's information without their permission. One aspect of privacy is the right of individuals to go about their daily activities, including home and work life, without having their personal information used against them. It's unlikely that Amazon will go out of its way to target people

Privacy, Data Harvesting, and You

The GDPR

On May 25, 2018, the European Union put into effect the General Data Protection Regulation (GDPR). It provides broad-ranging rules to allow people to keep their data private. The regulation requires companies, including social media firms, to obtain users' permission to collect their data. This permission is known as opt in. In contrast, in the United States, most data collection is opt out. In an opt-out approach, users' data is collected unless they specify that they don't want their data collected. The GDPR also restricts secondary uses of personal data. A secondary use is any purpose other than the one for which the user gave permission. For example, a user might agree that a retail company, such as Amazon, can use data about the products he or she purchases, to suggest related products. The company cannot use that data for any other purpose. In the United States, however, even when sites have a box that consumers must check to allow a company to collect their data, the use of that data is generally all or nothing. Checking the box allows the company to use the data collected for any purpose. The user's only recourse is not to check the box.

The GDPR also limits how companies can sort users into various groups. For instance, it might be considered improper to divide people into religious or ethnic groups, or economic classes, for the purposes of targeting selected groups with real estate ads because this practice is discriminatory. The regulation also gives users the right to know if they are sorted into groups, which groups, who is using the data, and for what purposes. If a user requests that his or her data be deleted, a company is required to do so. The GDPR makes it difficult for companies doing business in Europe to engage in the same type of data harvesting, data mining, and advertising practices they carry on in the United States. Indeed, many US users, including teens, would like to see the United States establish data protections similar to those of the GDPR. According to the website Kidscreen.com, 2018 research from the nonprofit organization Common Sense Media revealed that 69 percent of teens and 77 percent of parents think it is "'extremely important' for sites to ask permission before selling or sharing their personal information," and 97 percent of parents and 93 percent of teens believe it is at least moderately important.

for negative purposes. However, organizations that are less benign can harvest data for political reasons and stir up animosity toward particular groups, such as African Americans, Latinos, Muslims, or LGBTQ+ individuals.

The Right Not to Have Private Information Used Against You

A key factor in the right to privacy debate is the right for people not to have their personal information used against them. The Privacy Act of 1974 prohibits the government from compiling secret databases on American citizens. The Fourth Amendment asserts "the right of the people to be secure in their persons, houses, papers, and effects, against unreasonable searches and seizures." It requires that the government and its law enforcement agencies show probable cause that a crime has been committed and obtain a warrant to search a person's effects. This concept extends to a person's digital information. The collection of personal information by organizations has led to conflict between those organizations and the government. The government, in some situations, would like to search that data—for example, to locate threats to national security or to obtain evidence of a crime. The US government has

Privacy, Data Harvesting, and You

pressed companies such as Facebook, Google, Microsoft, Twitter, Uber, and Apple to share information about users. The government has routinely requested user information that isn't restricted to a particular suspect in a crime, but rather comprises thousands of users' records. In most cases, companies have refused to provide such access, or even to provide information on a particular suspect, without a court order requiring them to do so. However, the danger

The use of personal information to target consumers for product sales has become a widespread practice of both online and brick-and-mortar retailers, raising ethical concerns.

remains that some companies could decide to share personal data with government law enforcement agencies voluntarily.

The goal of the Privacy Act is to keep particular groups of citizens from being singled out for discrimination because of race, ethnicity, religion, or political affiliation. However, the act applies only to the government. It has no effect on the collection and analysis of personal data by corporations, retailers, or political or social policy groups. All of these types of organizations can collect data and use it in a variety of positive and negative ways. Retailers can use it to send ads for expensive goods or tickets to concerts and other activities to teens whose profiles indicate they come from affluent families. Political organizations can use it to send material encouraging people to vote for a specific candidate or to vote a certain way on a ballot question. Nonprofit organizations can use it to solicit donations based on particular demographic characteristics, such as socioeconomic status, race or ethnic group, or membership in particular organizations. Real estate agents could use it to send ads for desirable residences to individuals who fit particular economic, racial, or ethnic profiles—a potentially discriminatory practice.

CHAPTER 3

Online Consumer Nation

Increasingly, commerce is taking place online. Online commerce is done not only by companies, such as Amazon, that are known primarily as online retailers. Companies that once had just brick-and-mortar stores, such as Walmart, today have major online consumer operations. There are both advantages and disadvantages of data harvesting for consumers who patronize these retailers.

Why Harvest Data?

Businesses have embraced data harvesting and data mining because these processes allow them to identify relationships among purchases that they would otherwise be unable to find. The larger the pool of data, the easier it is for computer programs to find relationships. In other words, if one had data from one hundred teenagers of varying ethnicities, interests, and economic status, there might be great variation in what they purchase. However, if one has data from one hundred thousand teenagers, it is possible to see which items are most popular among teenagers, and to determine that a large percentage of them buy the same combination of items. This process also makes it possible to segment the teenagers into groups based on their demographic characteristics, such as gender, race, ethnicity, socioeconomic status, geographic location, and sexual orientation. This process allows marketers to further refine the marketing of products to them. Harvesting and mining data benefits companies in other ways as well. For example, it helps them to

Online Consumer Nation

Millennials are very interested in eating healthily, which is a focus of companies like Amazon, which bought grocer Whole Foods.

predict emerging trends. As new generations, such as millennials, become prominent, they have priorities and habits that are different from those of previous generations. Millennials are more interested in natural, organic foods than generation X or the baby boom generation and are more likely to have foods delivered. Also, as young people age, they are more likely to marry, start families, and set up households, requiring particular types of goods, from baby products to new furniture. Quickly identifying changes in consumer behavior—such as watching streaming video instead of cable or satellite television—enables companies to quickly adapt and offer new products to their customers.

Privacy, Data Harvesting, and You

The Do Not Track Kids Act

One of the areas of data harvesting and data mining that people find most alarming is the tracking of children's and teens' information and the marketing of products to them. The Do Not Track Kids bill, sponsored by Senator Ed Markey (Democrat from Massachusetts), was introduced into Congress on May 23, 2018. Its cosponsors are Senator Richard Blumenthal (Democrat from Connecticut) and Representatives Joe Barton (Republican from Texas) and Bobby Rush (Democrat from Illinois). The bill is designed to prevent companies from tracking the online activities of kids younger than sixteen years old. The Children's Online Privacy Protection Act, passed in 1998, protects children younger than thirteen by prohibiting companies from collecting their personal information, such as their geolocation and their activities on websites. The Do Not Track Kids Act would extend protection to teens under the age of sixteen. The bill is designed to prevent companies from engaging in advertising to teens, ages thirteen to fifteen, based on their online activities. It also requires companies to provide a means to delete some of the teens' personal information from their databases. The bill, as of December 2018, was in the first stage of the legislative process. It will be considered by a congressional committee that will decide whether or not to send it for a vote by Congress. Senator Markey had previously introduced a bill called the Do Not Track Kids Act of 2011, when he was a congressman, but the bill was not passed, nor was a similar bill that was proposed in 2015. Supporters of the act include the advocacy groups Common Sense Media, Campaign for Commercial-Free Childhood, and the Center for Digital Democracy. Companies have mounted strong opposition to the bill. They have found that tracking teens' online activities and then targeting advertising to them is their most effective way of marketing. Its restriction could have a negative impact on their revenues.

The Advantages of Harvesting Data

Data harvesting and data mining can make it easier for consumers to find products of interest and discover products that they might like. Prior to the advent of data mining, companies relied on surveys to find out what customers wanted. However, surveys are not always accurate. Sometimes what customers say they want is different from what they actually value most. For example, a supermarket survey might ask customers whether variety or price was more important to them. Many might say variety, but they actually choose to shop where the prices were cheapest, even if they have less choice (for example, Walmart rather than Kroger for groceries). In addition, the people who take the time to fill out a survey might not be representative of the overall pool of customers, or even the most desirable customers. The information acquired through data harvesting and mining allows companies to understand the real actions of customers and to provide them with products and features that they truly want. Targeting products to customers based on their previous purchases can be helpful because so many people, especially young people and millennials, use mobile devices such as smartphones and tablets to access websites. It can be difficult to type on a small device, so the fewer clicks, the better. If retailers know what items are most likely to interest a customer, they can show those items at the top of a list. This approach makes the shopping experience easy.

Privacy, Data Harvesting, and You

Teens are a lucrative market for retailers because they often have disposable income and few expenses, but parents and governments want to protect them from manipulation.

These processes also enable companies to offer consumers products that they might not be aware of. For example, if customers purchase combinations of products that indicate that they might be elderly, the company can show them other personal care or mobility aids that might help them. Data harvesting and mining allow companies to identify a user's patterns of behavior and interests. Therefore, if a purchase is made on a customer's account that seems out of whack with the type of purchases he or she usually makes, a computer algorithm can flag the transaction as possibly fraudulent. The company can then check with the customer to see if the transaction is legitimate. An elderly person might purchase a skateboard as a gift for a grandchild, but the purchase could also be a case of fraud. Fraudsters often begin their identify theft proceedings by making an inexpensive purchase of this type, to see if they can get away with it. By flagging such a purchase, the fraud detection algorithm allows companies to shut down credit card and bank accounts before fraudsters can bilk companies and consumers for thousands of dollars. Because the process of getting one's money back after identity theft can be time-consuming and aggravating, this flagging process helps consumers as well as companies.

The Drawbacks of Data Harvesting

Because data mining relies on big data, companies constantly acquire more data from a wide range of websites and databases. In time, companies can acquire so much data that they know people's age, gender, race or ethnicity, habits, likes, dislikes, religion, and sexual orientation, as well as where they reside, whether they have children, their bank account, credit card, Social Security numbers, and more. Not only have highly organized groups of hackers broken into organizational databases and stolen information, but also employees at corporations can run queries to acquire lists of people whom they could victimize.

Another issue with the collection and use of people's data is accuracy. Companies acquire data from different sources. The age of the data affects its accuracy. Over time, as people age and aspects of their lives are altered, their interests, activities, and situations change. However, the data stored in data warehouses doesn't always

Privacy, Data Harvesting, and You

Data breaches such as the one that occurred at Sony Corporation can give hackers access to user information they can use for identity theft or scams.

do so. The situation is made worse because companies that employ data mining have no way of knowing what data might be important. Therefore, they harvest every piece of data they can find about people. They typically collect data from a variety of different databases, and there is often conflicting data in these sources because data was entered at various times and for different reasons. Moreover, because it requires a long time to analyze the vast amount of data stored in data warehouses, even data that was accurate at the time it was collected might be out of date by the time the company uses it. Old and inaccurate data can create a false impression of consumers and lead to them being peppered with ads for products that are no longer of interest to them.

The computer algorithms keep track of people's purchases and interests by monitoring previous purchases and websites visited. They do not necessarily draw the correct conclusions from this information, however. This situation can result in annoying, irrelevant ads that pop up on every website one visits. A major reason for this happening is that the algorithms have no way of knowing why a purchase was made. If you purchase some books on the Civil War for a school paper you are writing, you are likely to get a slew of ads for other books on the topic long after the paper is turned in. Likewise, if you use a website to purchase a baby product for your sister's baby shower, you are liable to get endless ads for baby (or even pregnancy) products for a long time to come. The situation

Online Consumer Nation

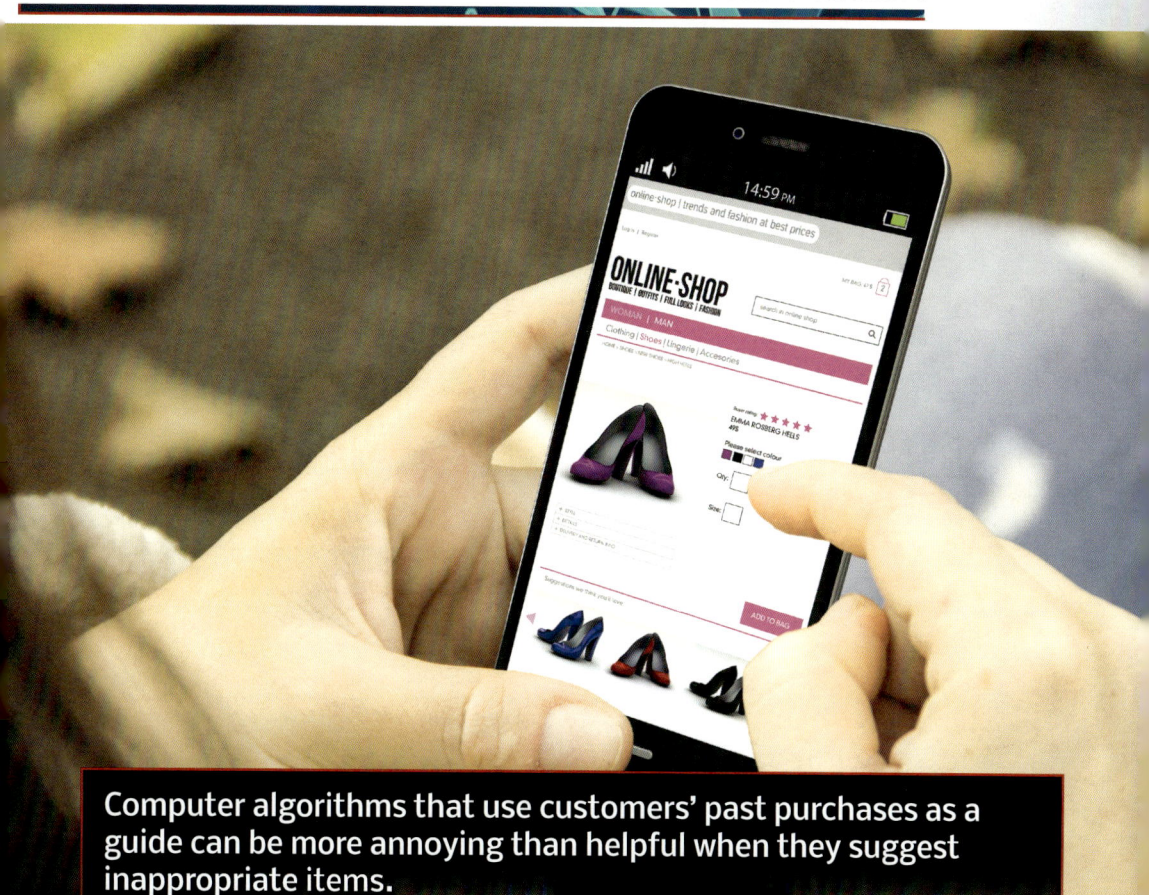

Computer algorithms that use customers' past purchases as a guide can be more annoying than helpful when they suggest inappropriate items.

gets even worse if the company sells your data to other companies or shares it with marketing partners.

One quandary faced by companies is that data harvesting has led to the collection of so much data—and data mining has become so sophisticated—that it is possible for a company to identify people who are likely to have serious medical problems. In some cases, the person may not be aware of the problem. What should a company do if an algorithm reveals that a customer might have a disease such as diabetes, Alzheimer's disease, or clinical depression? Should it inform the person? If it does so, he or she might be upset that the company has unearthed this information. But would it be ethical for the company to ignore the situation?

CHAPTER 4

The Power of Persuasion

Data harvesting can be used to identify potential voters likely to support a candidate so that legitimate advertising can be sent to individuals of the candidate's party to encourage them to vote. It can also be used to identify people who are undecided or of the opposite party. These people can then be targeted to persuade them to change their vote or to convince them that the candidate in question shares their views on particular issues. In a similar way, individuals of particular ethnicities, races, genders, or with particular sexual orientations could be sent advertising that explains how a particular candidate best supports their interests. This type of targeted political advertising has been around as long as there has been voting. People might object to the fact that political organizations have access to their data, but the concept of political advertising is not new—it has merely adopted new technology. However, the internet provides an avenue for undermining rather than supporting democracy, on a scale that has not previously existed.

Data Harvesting and Politics

On February 16, 2018, the US Justice Department indicted thirteen Russians for interfering in the 2016 US presidential elections via social media sites such as Facebook and Twitter. Twelve of those arrested worked for the Internet Research Agency, a Russian intelligence organization with ties to Russian president Vladimir Putin. The

The Power of Persuasion

This Facebook page for a group called Being Patriotic provides an example of the sites set up by Russian intelligence to influence the 2016 US presidential election.

Russians set up a virtual computer network (VCN), a computer system that remotely controls a computer in another location. The Russian VCN had an internet address in the United States, to make it look as if its social media accounts were located in the United States.

Hundreds of people employed by the Internet Research Agency were involved in the effort, and the agency spent millions of dollars to accomplish their goal of influencing the election. They were spending roughly $1,250,000 per week by September 2016, according to the indictment. The Russian agents created hundreds of social media accounts for fictitious people whom they attempted to turn into opinion leaders. They targeted a range of issues, including race and immigration. They acquired hundreds of thousands of followers. The malefactors disparaged Hillary Clinton, who was known to have strong opposition to Russian policies, as well as candidates competing with Donald Trump for the Republican nomination, such as Ted Cruz and Marco Rubio. They threw support behind Bernie Sanders and then Donald Trump, organizing rallies in support of these candidates as well as attempting to influence people's opinions. The Russian government wished to keep Hillary Clinton from becoming president because she was an opponent of many Russian activities and policies and was likely to take actions to oppose them. As the election approached, they worked to discourage minorities from voting because the Russians believed they were more likely to vote for Hillary Clinton.

In September 2017, social media companies began to realize that some political ads on their sites were funded by Russia. They informed federal authorities, leading to a Federal Bureau of Investigation (FBI) investigation and the appointment of a special counsel at the Justice Department. The Russian conspirators attempted to destroy evidence of their activities, but thirteen of them were arrested. According to a CBS News report, one, Viktorovna Kaverzina, sent an email to her family, stating, "I created all these pictures and posts, and the Americans believed that it was written by their people."

Contributing to the success of the Russian efforts were data bubbles (also known as filter bubbles). Many search algorithms provide recommended sites and information to users based on their previously visited pages, which reveal their interests. Thus, users tend to see only pages or posts that support what they already believe, rather than a wide range of pages or posts that may offer different viewpoints and information. This limited access to information and opinion can present users with a distorted view of events and make certain viewpoints and activities seem very dramatic.

On August 24, 2018, the *New York Times* reported that Microsoft had found and shut down fraudulent sites that were imitating those of two conservative American think tanks. According to the

The Power of Persuasion

Facebook, Google, and Twitter executives testify before the Senate Judiciary Committee on October 31, 2017, about attempts by Russia to interfere in the 2016 US election.

New York Times, the fake sites were "created by hackers linked to a Russian military intelligence unit, [and] indicated that the Kremlin was widening its attacks beyond deceiving voters." A day after the Microsoft announcement, Facebook revealed that it had removed 652 fraudulent accounts. It stated that the pages and groups that were trying to spread disinformation were aimed not only at the United States, but also at Britain, Latin America, and the Middle East. The company also stated that Iran was emerging as another agent attempting to create false information.

Privacy, Data Harvesting, and You

The Facebook Data-Sharing Scandal

In 2018, Facebook was embroiled in a data-usage scandal when it was revealed that the data the company collected and shared with Cambridge Analytica had been used for political purposes. The practice began in 2013, when application developer Aleksandr Kogan created a personality quiz for Facebook. Kogan used the app to access the data of millions of people and then shared the data with Cambridge Analytica. Cambridge Analytica used the data without Facebook's permission to target voters in the 2016 US presidential election.

As a result of the ensuing scandal, Facebook is placing limitations on the data that apps can collect. Apps will be prohibited from gathering data about users' friends without their permission. In addition, developers are now required to receive approval from Facebook before they can request sensitive data from users. Facebook is also auditing apps that they feel are engaging in suspicious activity and taking steps to help users better control which applications access their data.

Many users were upset by the data misuse by Cambridge Analytica, and some people deleted their Facebook accounts. However, the majority of users have kept their accounts. Facebook chief executive officer Mark Zuckerberg and chief operating officer Sheryl Sandberg have testified before Congress regarding the scandal and the steps they are taking to prevent further misappropriation of data.

The Power of Persuasion

The Potential for Abuse

Businesses are not the only organizations interested in people's activities. The government and law enforcement have a vested interest in the personal data collected by social media, telephone, and other companies. In many cases, companies resist sharing data with the government unless they receive a court order in relation to a specific crime. Nonetheless, the government is pressuring companies to share their harvested data. The government's position is that monitoring people's activity—such as their phone records—could help identify patterns of behavior that indicate a person might be a threat to national security. But not all people who fit such a pattern present a threat to the United States.

Agencies such as the FBI and Department of Homeland Security engaging in probes often attempt to obtain data collected by companies on individuals. The heads of some of the intelligence agencies are seen here at a hearing before the Senate Intelligence Committee.

Privacy, Data Harvesting, and You

Law enforcement agencies are also interested in accessing that data. Data harvesting and mining could be used to identify the characteristics of people who are likely to participate in illegal activity. However, the algorithms used to identify such potential criminals are often discriminatory, singling out people with specific racial and socioeconomic characteristics. Further, algorithms that use incarcerated people and their characteristics as a model for potential criminals are likely to find a high number of false positives—law-abiding people who happen to share certain demographic characteristics with some incarcerated people. They will also miss a large number of potential criminals who do not fit the profile of the algorithm. They will certainly miss criminals who engage in crimes that have arisen as a result of new technologies, such as stealing money in bitcoin accounts or locking up a company's computers and demanding blackmail money to unlock them.

Above all, such routine monitoring of citizens for suspicious activity is forbidden by the Fourth Amendment, which covers "The right of the people to be secure in their persons, houses, papers, and effects, against unreasonable searches and seizures." The Fourth Amendment requires that the government and its law enforcement agencies show probable cause that a crime has been committed and obtain a warrant to search a person's property. If the government or federal or local law enforcement agencies use data harvested by companies, they are violating the protections guaranteed by the Constitution. These protections are designed to ensure people's freedom and allow them to live without fear of government interference. Moreover, a person who meets the criteria for engaging in suspicious activity may not be planning to do anything wrong or may change his or her mind and not commit the act. This type of government surveillance limits the freedom of people and causes everyone stress. It makes them worry that anything they do might be misinterpreted. In the worst case, the government or other organizations could use such data to target and persecute

The Power of Persuasion

specific groups of people, such as those of a particular race, ethnicity, sexual orientation, religion, or gender identity.

Because data harvesting reveals personal characteristics of people, it can be misused in ways that result in either deliberate or unintentional discrimination. For example, it provides information that could be used in a way that violates hiring and housing laws and regulations. When interviewing candidates for jobs, potential employers are forbidden to ask about religion, ethnicity, or marital status (a person's marital status could be used to eliminate women who might leave to have children). However, data harvesting and mining applications provide this information. Similarly, real estate agents could use race, socioeconomic status, age, or other personal information to select clients for rental properties in certain areas, in violation of the law.

Data harvesting and mining allow companies to identify those who are well educated and affluent, giving them preferential treatment and ignoring people of lower socioeconomic status. For example, data harvesting and mining combined with automated computer-based risk analysis are sometimes used to decide who gets a mortgage or loan and who doesn't. This approach can

Many banks and lending institutions use computer algorithms to analyze data and make the decision whether or not to issue individuals loans.

Privacy, Data Harvesting, and You

lead to discrimination against the less affluent. Many companies have come to rely on computer applications to make decisions such as these, with little or no human discretion. Companies need to put policies in place that guarantee that they are not engaging in discrimination that is both illegal and unethical.

It is easy to use harvesting data to reveal the actual or likely political leaning, race, religion, and sexual orientation of individuals. This information could be misused by hate groups and governments that wish to target specific groups of people today or in the future.

CHAPTER 5

Protecting Your Data

Data harvesting and mining are a reality everyone has to live with. Only public laws can control the collection and use of data on a large scale. However, there are a number of steps that individuals can take to protect their privacy and reduce access to their data.

Controlling Access to Your Data

A *Time* magazine article, "11 Simple Ways to Protect Your Privacy," recommends a number of steps you can take to protect your personal data. Several of these are discussed below.

Don't put sensitive personal information in your social media profile. Don't include your birthdate, phone number, and the like in any social media profiles. Avoid giving out your Social Security number. The only companies that need it are your employer, your bank, and the Internal Revenue Service (IRS). Use the private browsing option on your browser when using the internet on your smartphone or tablet. This setting deletes cookies and other browsing information when you close your browser. Be aware that the Twitter, Google+, Facebook, and other social media buttons included on webpages allow those companies to track your activity, regardless of whether you have an account or are logged in. Delete cookies regularly using the tools on your browser. Doing so will

Privacy, Data Harvesting, and You

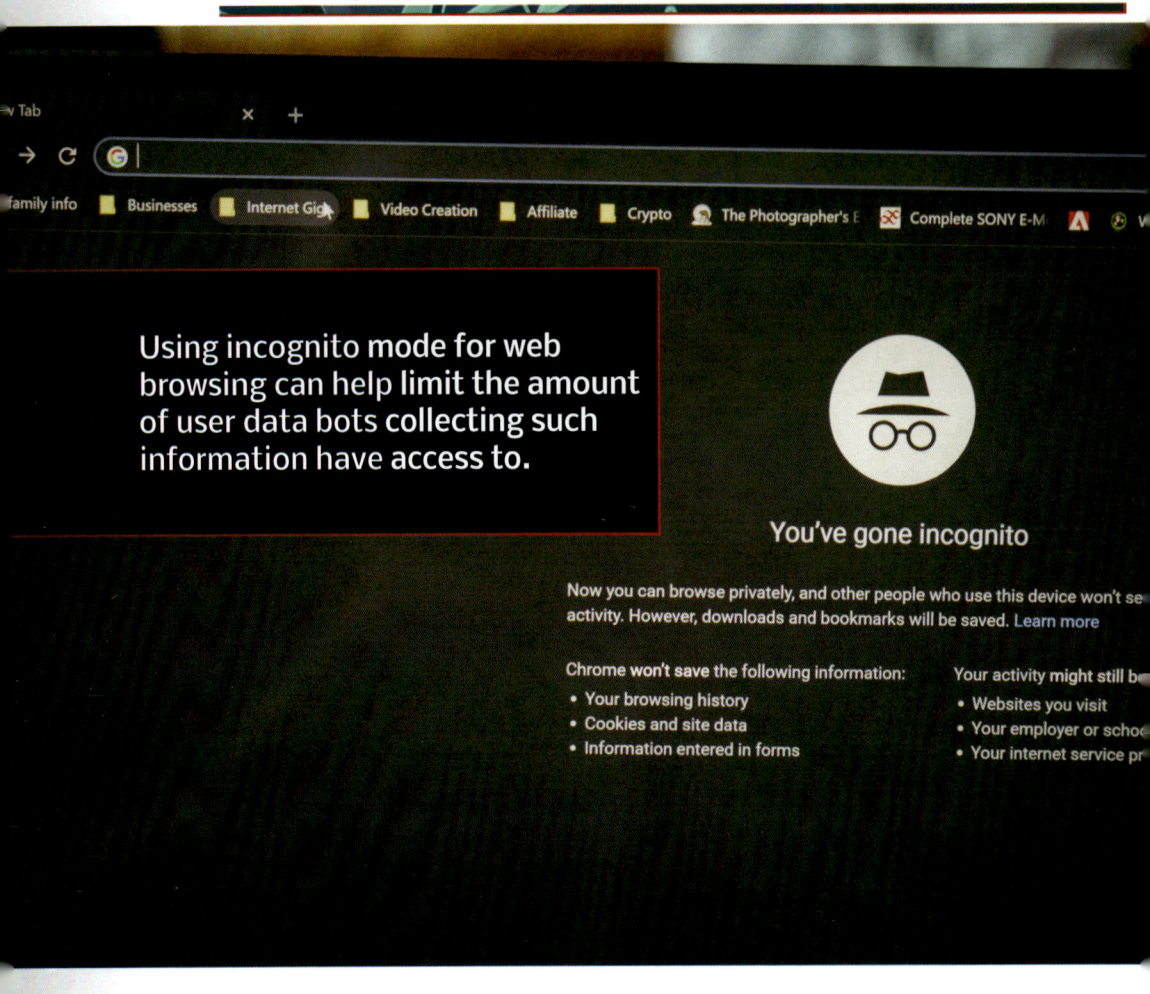

> Using incognito mode for web browsing can help limit the amount of user data bots collecting such information have access to.

not only reduce the number of companies tracking your data, but will also speed up your device.

Use different passwords for different sites—especially those where you carry out financial transactions, such as your bank's online site or Amazon. That way, if an identity thief gets hold of one password, he or she can't use it to access all the sites where you do business. If you can't remember multiple passwords, use a password vault or manager app to store them. Also, many sites that are involved in financial transactions or that store personal data—such as Facebook, Apple, Microsoft, credit card companies, and others—give you the option of using two-factor authentication. With this type of identification,

Protecting Your Data

you first put in your password and then the company sends a special code to your phone, which you enter to verify your identity. This process takes a little more time, but if you choose to use this option, a hacker can't get access to your account with your password alone.

Check your settings on social media sites, such as Facebook, Twitter, Instagram, and others, and adjust the privacy setting options to make sure only friends or followers can see your posts. If you have the option of turning off a setting that lets people see your geographical location, do so. This setting can be used for negative purposes, from the merely annoying (such as sending you recommendations for a restaurant where you're already eating) to the downright dangerous (such as enabling a person to stalk you or rob your home because your location makes it obvious that you're out of town). Google gives you the option of setting up an alert that lets you know when someone is referring to you online. Google lets you choose what to search for, on which types of web pages, and how often.

Avoid giving your phone number or zip code when you purchase items in a store. If you do, it will be entered into a database and can be used by employees or hackers, along with the name on your account or credit card, to find your address. Similarly, use fake information when setting up security questions on online accounts. The purpose of such security questions is simply to verify that you should have access to your account if you forget your password or are logging in from an unfamiliar computer. It doesn't matter if the answer is true or not, just that it agrees with what you entered before.

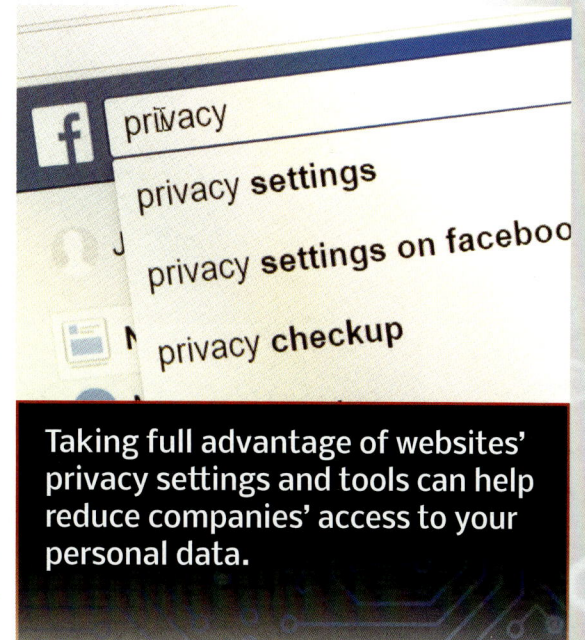

Taking full advantage of websites' privacy settings and tools can help reduce companies' access to your personal data.

43

Privacy, Data Harvesting, and You

The California Consumer Privacy Act of 2018

In June 2018, California passed a landmark privacy law, the California Consumer Privacy Act of 2018. The law is similar to the GDPR passed by the European Union but differs in some

State Senator Bob Hertzberg (D-Van Nuys) speaks during the state senate session during which lawmakers approved the California Consumer Privacy Act of 2018.

Protecting Your Data

specifics. Under this law, companies are required to disclose the type of data they collect and to let users opt out of having their data sold. The law was passed despite the efforts of companies such as Amazon and AT&T, which spent millions of dollars to oppose it. It takes effect in 2020.

The California Consumer Privacy Act hits the heart of many internet companies' revenue, which is based on selling advertising to targeted users. As a result, many major tech companies— including Facebook, Google, IBM, and Microsoft— are lobbying the Trump administration to pass a federal privacy law that would supersede the state law. These companies feel that such a federal law would be more lenient than the California law. Because some form of regulation regarding privacy is probably inevitable, they want to have a role in creating it so that it will have less of a negative effect on their business.

For example, when you are asked for your mother's maiden name, you can enter her real maiden name or Rumpelstiltskin. All you need to do is remember what name to enter if the question appears in the future. Using fake information for questions such as mother's maiden name, city where you were born, the name of your high school, and the like keeps hackers from being able to use information from public records about you to hack your accounts.

What You Can Do

Practicing online safety can help protect your data. Beyond that, you can support state and federal efforts to enact laws that restrict the collection and use of data via data harvesting. Such regulation

Privacy, Data Harvesting, and You

When teens work to get out the vote or gain support for causes like data privacy, they help change the manner in which companies behave and the way Congress regulates them.

should require companies to inform users of what is collected about them. It should also give them an option not to have their data collected and used. Email your congressperson and senators and let them know you want them to support such bills. Vote, if you are old enough, or encourage your parents and older siblings to do so. If the ballot in your state includes a referendum about such a bill, take the time to go to the polls and vote in favor of it, or encourage others to do so. Also, consider whether it's worth paying a small fee to avoid having your data collected and used for advertising purposes. When the streaming service Hulu started offering an alternative to its advertising-supported free service, for a monthly fee of about $12, it turned out to be quite popular. Social media companies believe that if they charge for using their service, users will leave. Therefore, they collect data to share with advertisers who pay for ads on the site. If you would be willing to support a paid alternative, let the company know, through their forums or via email. Strong public and private efforts are required if people want to control how, when, and for what purpose their data is used.

Glossary

advocacy Supporting, promoting, or acting for the good of a cause.

affluent Financially well off; having a lot of money and financial assets.

aggregate To collect from various sources.

algorithm Computer code containing a set of steps for solving a particular problem.

auditing Reviewing the records of the activities of a person, company, or computer application.

benign Harmless.

big data Vast amounts of data collected by companies and stored in databases.

bitcoin A form of computer-based currency used for electronic financial transactions.

bot A small piece of code that searches through data and collects data.

cookie A piece of code inserted by an organization or company onto a person's computer in order to track their online activities.

data warehouse A repository of very large amounts of collected data.

demographic Personal information such as age, race, gender, and the like that is used to segment people into groups.

disinformation False information created to deliberately mislead people.

disparage To belittle or make someone look bad in the eyes of others.

dubious Doubtful or questionable.

Glossary

ethnicity The cultural group to which one belongs, such as Hispanic or Asian.

extract To take or pull out.

fast data A method of analyzing data in real time as a user interacts with a website.

fraudulent Fake, deliberately misleading, or designed to trick people.

hepatitis A disease that causes problems with the liver.

illicit Illegal.

incarcerated Confined to a prison.

indictment A list of charges brought by a law enforcement agency against a person suspected of a crime.

Internet Protocol (IP) address A series of numbers that identify a computer connected to the internet.

inundated Flooded with.

legitimate True and legal.

machine learning A type of artificial intelligence that allows data mining software to improve the accuracy of its algorithms by altering them without human intervention.

malefactor A person who commits a crime or unethical act.

malignant Causing harm, suffering, or distress.

misappropriation Illegal collection and usage.

patent database A computer file of a company's legally protected product designs.

Privacy, Data Harvesting, and You

proprietary Describing a product, service, or process that is unique to a particular company, which controls the rights to use or sell it.

quandary A dilemma; a situation in which a person is uncertain what to do.

recourse Access to protection.

referendum A question on a ballot used to measure the amount of voter support for a proposed government regulation.

script A piece of computer code that performs a specific function.

server A large-capacity computer that runs a computer network.

socioeconomic Relating to one's financial status and social class.

supersede To replace.

think tank An organization consisting of a group of people who come together to share ideas to solve problems or achieve particular goals.

two-factor authentication A form of online identity verification that requires a special code sent to a user's phone in addition to a password.

virtual computer network A computer system that remotely controls a computer in another location.

white-hat hacker A person who hacks computer systems for positive rather than negative purposes, such as tracking down a group stealing data.

For More Information

American Civil Liberties Union (ACLU)

125 Broad Street, 18th Floor
New York, NY 10004
(212) 549-2500
Website: http://www.aclu.org/issues/privacy-technology
Facebook and Twitter: @ACLU
Besides defending and safeguarding people's rights and freedoms, the ACLU works to protect citizen's privacy and their control over their personal data.

Center for Democracy and Technology (CDT)

Tower Building
1401 K Street NW, Suite 200
Washington, DC 20005
(202) 637-9800
Website: https://cdt.org
Facebook and Twitter: @CenDemTech
CDT is a nonprofit organization that advocates for regulations, nationally and internationally, that protect the rights of individuals with regard to privacy and technology.

Constitution Project: Data Collection and Privacy

1200 18th Street NW, Suite 1000
Washington, DC, 20036
(202) 580-6920
Website: https://constitutionproject.org/issues/rule-of-law/data-collection-privacy
Facebook: @ConstitutionProject

Twitter: @ConPro
The Constitution Project's mission is to bring together people of diverse viewpoints to arrive at solutions to Constitution-related issues, including those involving privacy and data collection.

Department of Justice Canada

275 Sparks Street, 9th Floor
Ottawa, ON K1A 0H8
Canada
(613) 907-3700
Website: http://www.justice.gc.ca/eng/trans/atip-aiprp
Facebook and Twitter: @JusticeCanadaEn or @JusticeCanadaFr
The Department of Justice is the agency of the Canadian government responsible for enforcing the Privacy Act and provides online information on protecting privacy and one's identity.

Electronic Privacy Information Center (EPIC)

1718 Connecticut Avenue NW, Suite 200
Washington, DC 20009
(202) 483-1140
Website: http://www.epic.org/privacy
Facebook: @epicprivacy
Twitter: @EPICPrivacy
EPIC focuses public attention on privacy and civil liberties issues, works to promote the public's influence in decisions concerning the future of the internet, and runs the Consumer Privacy Project, which advocates with the US government on behalf of consumers.

For More Information

Office of the Privacy Commissioner of Canada

30 Victoria Street
Gatineau, QC K1A 1H3
Canada
(819) 994-5444 or (800) 282-1376
Website: http://www.priv.gc.ca/en/contact-the-opc
Facebook: @PrivCanada
Twitter: @PrivacyPrivee (English) or @PriveePrivacy (French)
This office provides the latest information on attempts to control privacy and on how to protect one's data and identity in Canada.

For Further Reading

Brown, Meta S. *Data Mining for Dummies*. Hoboken, NJ: John Wiley, 2014.

Eboch, M. M., ed. *Data Mining* (Introducing Issues with Opposing Views). New York, NY: Greenhaven Publishing, 2018.

Francis, Leslie, and John G. Francis. *Privacy: What Everyone Needs to Know*. New York, NY: Oxford University Press, 2017.

Freedman, Jeri. *When Companies Spy on You: Corporate Data Mining and Big Business* (Spying, Surveillance, and Privacy in the 21st Century). New York, NY: Cavendish Square, 2018.

Furgang, Kathy. *Internet Surveillance and How to Protect Your Privacy* (Digital Information Literacy). New York, NY: Rosen Publishing, 2017.

Goodman, Marc. *Future Crimes: Inside the Digital Underground and the Battle for Our Connected World*. New York, NY: Anchor Press, 2016.

Hartzog, Woodrow. *Privacy's Blueprint: The Battle to Control the Design of New Technologies*. Cambridge, MA: Harvard University Press, 2018.

Johanson, Paula, ed. *Filter Bubbles* (Opposing Viewpoints). New York, NY: Greenhaven Publishing, 2018.

Kyi, Tanya Lloyd. *Eyes & Spies: How You're Tracked and Why You Should Know*. Berkeley, CA: Annick Press, 2017.

Lusted, Marcia Amidon, ed. *Hacking and Freedom of Information* (Opposing Viewpoints). New York, NY: Greenhaven Publishing, 2018.

Moretta, Alison. *How to Maintain Your Privacy Online* (Web Wisdom). New York, NY: Cavendish Square, 2015.

For Further Reading

O'Neil, Cathy. *Weapons of Math Destruction: How Big Data Increases Inequality and Threatens Democracy*. New York, NY: Broadway Books, 2017.

Wacks, Raymond. *Privacy: A Very Short Introduction*. 2nd ed. New York, NY: Oxford University Press, 2015.

Wilcox, Christine. *Thinking Critically: Online Privacy* (Thinking Critically). San Diego, CA: ReferencePoint Press, 2015.

Wilkinson, Colin. *Everything You Need to Know About Digital Privacy* (The Need to Know Library). New York, NY: Rosen Publishing, 2018.

Bibliography

Abusix. "A Brief History of Bots and How They Shaped the Internet Today." September 21, 2016. https://www.abusix.com/blog/a-brief-history-of-bots-and-how-theyve-shaped-the-internet-today.

Anderson, Monica, and Jingjing Jiang. "Teens, Social Media & Technology 2018." Pew Research Center, May 31, 2018. http://www.pewinternet.org/2018/05/31/teens-social-media-technology-2018.

Aycock, Jason. "Facing New Rules, Techs Press for Federal Privacy Law." Seeking Alpha, August 27, 2018. https://seekingalpha.com/news/3385839-facing-new-rules-techs-press-federal-privacy-law.

Borocas, Solon. "Losing Out on Employment Because of Big Data Mining." *New York Times*, August 8, 2014. https://www.nytimes.com/roomfordebate/2014/08/06/is-big-data-spreading-inequality/losing-out-on-employment-because-of-big-data-mining.

BrightPlanet. "How We Do Data Harvesting." May 16, 2017. https://brightplanet.com/2017/05/how-we-do-data-harvesting.

CBS News. "Read the Social Media Posts Russians Allegedly Used to Influence 2016 Election Cycle." February 16, 2018. https://www.cbsnews.com/news/read-social-media-posts-russians-allegedly-used-to-influence-the-election.

CBS News. "Rod Rosenstein Announced Indictments of Russians in U.S. Election Meddling." February 16, 2018. https://www.cbsnews.com/news/russian-indictment-2016-elections-rod-rosenstein-announcement-today-2018-02-16.

Davis, Wendy. "Lawmakers Push to Ban Behavioral Targeting of Kids under 16." Digital News Daily, May 24, 2018. https://

Bibliography

www.mediapost.com/publications/article/319752/lawmakers -push-to-ban-behavioral-targeting-of-kids.html.

DesMarinas, Christina. "11 Simple Ways to Protect Your Privacy." *Time*, July 24, 2013. http://techland.time.com/2013/07/24/11 -simple-ways-to-protect-your-privacy.

Duhigg, Charles. "How Companies Learn Your Secrets." *New York Times Magazine*, February 16, 2012. https://www.nytimes .com/2012/02/19/magazine/shopping-habitshtml?r=1&ref =charlesduhigg.

Dwoskin, Elizabeth. "EU Data-Privacy Law Raises Daunting Prospects for US Companies." *Wall Street Journal*, December 16, 2015. http://www.wsj.com./articles/eu-data-privacy-law -raises-daunting-prospects-for-u-s-companies-1450306033.

Hill, Kashmir. "How Target Figured Out a Teen Girl Was Pregnant Before Her Father Did." *Forbes*, February 16, 2016. https://www.forbes.com/sites/kashmirhill/2012/02/16/how -target-figured-out-a-teen-girl-was-pregnant-before-her -father-did/#6be1a6ec6668.

Kadlec, Dan. "Privacy? Here's How Data Mining Might Actually Help Consumers." *Time*, March 6, 2012. http://business.time .com/2012/03/06/privacy-heres-how-data-mining-might -actually-help-consumers.

Kaufman, Roy. "How Traders Are Using Text and Data Mining to Beat the Market." The Street, February 12, 2015. https://www .thestreet.com/story/13044694/2/how-traders-are-using-text -and-data-mining-to-beat-the-market.html.

Kidscreen.com. "Common Sense Finds Social Media Privacy Matters to Teens." June 11, 2018. http://kidscreen .com/2018/06/11/common-sense-finds-social-media -privacy-matters-to-teens.

Privacy, Data Harvesting, and You

Koutoupis, Petros. "Data Privacy: Why It Matters and How to Protect Yourself." *Linux Journal*, June 5, 2018. https://www.linuxjournal.com/content/data-privacy-why-it-matters-and-how-protect-yourself.

Lecher, Colin. "California Just Passed One of the Toughest Data Privacy Laws in the Country." The Verge, June 28, 2018. https://www.theverge.com/2018/6/28/17509720/california-consumer-privacy-act-legislation-law-vote.

Lee, Choong Ho, and Hyung-Jin Yoon. "Medical Big Data: Promise and Challenges." *Kidney Research and Clinical Practice*, March 2017. Volume 36(1), pp 3–11. https://www.ncbi.nlm.nih.gov/pmc/articles/PMC5331970.

Make Use Of. "10 Real Examples of When Data Harvesting Exposed Your Data." May 24, 2018. https://www.makeuseof.com/tag/data-harvesting-personal-info.

Marr, Bernard. "Big Data: 20 Mind-Boggling Facts Everyone Must Read." *Forbes*, September 30, 2015. http://www.forbes.com/sites/bernardmarr/2015/09/30/big-data-20-mind-boggling-facts-everyone-must-read/#2d3918556c1d.

Marr, Bernard. "How Big Data Is Transforming Medicine." *Forbes*, February 16, 2016. https://www.forbes.com/sites/bernardmarr/2016/02/16/how-big-data-is-transforming-medicine/#5fe568e67ddc.

Marr, Bernard. "17 Predictions about the Future of Big Data Everyone Should Read." *Forbes*, March 15, 2016. http://www.forbes.com/sites/bernardmarr/2016/03/15/17-predictions-about-the-future-of-big-data-everyone-should-read/#6aabf2dd157c.

McFarland, Matt. "The Incredible Potential and Dangers of Data Mining Health Records." *Washington Post*, October 14, 2014.

Bibliography

https://www.washingtonpost.com/news/innovations/wp/2014/10/01/the-incredible-potential-and-dangers-of-data-mining-health-records/?utm_term=.03a5680b2d83.

Oracle Corporation. "Data Mining Concepts." Oracle Help Center. Retrieved August 27, 2018. https://docs.oracle.com/cd/B28359_01/datamine.111/b28129/process.htm#DMCON002.

Parrack, Dave. "Facebook Addresses the Cambridge Analytica Scandal." MUD Tech News, March 22, 2018. https://www.makeuseof.com/tag/facebook-cambridge-analytica-scandal.

Pasierbinska-Wilson, Zuzanna. "When Data Collection Goes Wrong: 10 Examples of Identity Data Being Misused." *Target Marketing*, January 13, 2016. http://www.targetmarketingmag.com/article/when-data-collection-goes-wrong-10-examples-identity-data-being-misused/all.

Rossi, Ben. "How Common Is Insider Misuse—and How Can It Be Neutralized?" *Information Age*, September 20, 2016. http://www.information-age.com/common-insider-misuse-123462235.

Scheer, Robert. *They Know Everything About You: How Data-Collecting Corporations and Snooping Government Agencies Are Destroying Democracy*. New York, NY: Nation Books, 2015.

Schneier, Bruce. *Data and Goliath: The Hidden Battles to Collect Your Data and Control Your World*. New York, NY: W. W. Norton, 2015.

Schwartz, Sarah. "YouTube Accused of Targeting Children with Ads, Violating Federal Privacy Law." *Education Week*, April 13, 2018. https://blogs.edweek.org/edweek/DigitalEducation/2018/04/youtube_targeted_ads_coppa_complaint.html.

Singer, Natasha. "The Week in Tech: Democracy Under Siege," *New York Times*, August 24, 2018, https://www.nytimes.com/2018/08/24/technology/week-in-tech-democracy-siege.html.

Singer, P. W., and Allan Friedman. *Cybersecurity and Cyberwar: What Everyone Needs to Know*. New York, NY: Oxford University Press, 2014.

University of Cambridge Psychometrics Research Centre & Edelman. *Trust and Predictive Technologies 2016*. Edelman Insights. Retrieved August 26, 2018. https://www.slideshare.net/EdelmanInsights/trust-predictive-technologies-2016.

Index

A
accuracy, of data, 27, 29, 30
advantages of harvesting data, 24, 27–29
advertising, 18
  effect of GDPR on, 20
  paying fees to avoid, 47
  political, 32
  selling of, 16
  targeted, 7, 15, 45
  teens as target for, 18, 20–21
advocacy groups, 26
age, and data harvesting, 4, 26, 29, 39
aggregators, data, 9, 10
algorithms, 13, 14, 29, 30, 31, 38
  fraud detection, 29
  search, 34
  used by law enforcement, 38
Amazon, 13, 19, 20, 21, 24, 42, 45
Apple, 21–22, 42
auditing
  of apps, 36
  of logs, 10

B
big data, 11, 13, 29
bitcoin accounts, 38
bots
  attempts to gain access by, 12
  and collecting information, 4, 9
  definition of, 4, 7
BrightPlanet, 9–10

C
California Consumer Privacy Act of 2018, 44–45
Cambridge Analytica, 8, 36
captcha, 12, 13
Children's Online Privacy Protection Act, 26
Clinton, Hillary, 34
Common Sense Media, 21, 26
Congress, 6, 26, 36
Constitution, 16, 38
cookies, 41

D
data warehouses, 13, 29–30
decision support systems, 11
democracy, and the internet, 32
discrimination, 20, 23, 38, 39–40
disinformation, 35
Do Not Track Kids Act, 26–27
drawbacks, of data harvesting, 29–31

E
election, Russian interference in US, 32, 33, 34, 36

61

ethnicity
  and data harvesting, 4, 20, 24, 29, 32, 38–39
  discrimination based on, 23
European Union, 20, 44–45

F

Facebook, 8, 16, 21–22, 32, 35, 41, 42, 43, 45
  data-sharing scandal, 36
fast data mining, 13
financial data, 13
financial transactions, 4, 13, 42
Fourth Amendment, 21, 38

G

gender, and data harvesting, 4, 24, 29, 32
gender identity, 38–39
General Data Protection Regulation (GDPR), 20–21, 44–45
Google, 21–22, 43, 45
government, and data harvesting, 6, 11, 20, 21–23, 34, 37, 38–39, 40
governmental regulation, 6, 39, 45–46
Grindr, 8–9

H

hacking, 7, 10, 11, 12, 29, 35, 43, 45
health, and data harvesting, 4, 6, 11

hepatitis, 18
HIV status, 9

I

identity theft, 7, 10, 12, 29
incarcerated people, 38
Instagram, 16, 43
Internet Research Agency, 32–33
IP address, 9–10

L

law enforcement, 21, 22–23, 37, 38
loan, 6, 39

M

machine learning, 4, 6
medical data, 11
medical problems, discovered through data mining, 11, 31
Medicare, 11
Microsoft, 21–22, 34–35, 42, 45
millennials, 25, 27
misappropriation, of data, 36
mortgage, 6, 39

P

passwords, 42–43
patent databases, 10
permission, to collect data, 4, 7, 19, 20, 21, 36
Pole, Andrew, 14, 15
politics, and data harvesting, 6, 18, 21, 23, 32–35, 36, 40

Index

portal dashboard, 9
Privacy Act of 1974, 21, 23
proprietary company information, 10
protection, of data, 6, 20–21, 41, 45
Putin, Vladimir, 32–33

Q
quandary, of data harvesting, 31

R
real estate agents, 20, 23, 39
retailers, online, 20, 23, 24
  collection of data by, 23
  targeting of customers, 13, 27
  teens targeted by, 18

S
script 4, 7, 13
servers, 7, 9–10
sexual orientation, and data harvesting, 4, 18, 24, 29, 32, 38–39, 40
smartphone, use of, 16, 27, 41
Snapchat, 16
social media, 10, 16, 17–18, 20, 32, 33–34, 37, 41, 43, 47
Social Security numbers, 7, 29, 41
socioeconomic status, and data harvesting, 4, 23, 24, 38, 39
SSNDOB, 10, 12
surveys, 4, 6, 27

T
Target, 13, 14, 15
targeting
  of advertising, 7, 45
  Amazon, 19, 21
  criminals, 18, 27
  of customers, 13, 16
  emails, 7
  of government, 38–39, 40
  for real estate, 20
  of teens, 18, 26–27
  of voters, 32, 34, 36
think tanks, 34–35
third parties, and data, 8, 13, 18
Trump, Donald, 34
  administration, 45
Trust and Predictive Technologies 2016, 6
Twitter, 16, 21–22, 32, 41, 43
two-factor authentication, 42

U
US Justice Department, 32, 34

V
virtual computer network (VCN), 33
voting, 23, 32, 34, 35, 36, 46–47

W
white-hat hackers, 10

Z
Zuckerberg, Mark, 36

About the Author

Jeri Freedman has a bachelor's degree from Harvard University. She worked at high-technology companies for fifteen years. She is the author of numerous nonfiction books, including *America Debates: Privacy vs. Security*; *Careers in Computer Science and Programming*; *Online Safety*; and *Software Development*.

Photo Credits

Cover (padlock and eye graphic) Photographer is my life/Moment/Getty Images; pp. 4–5 Caroline Purser/Photographer's Choice/Getty Images; pp. 8–9 Gorodenkoff/Shutterstock.com; pp. 10, 34–35 Chip Somodevilla/Getty Images; p. 12 metrue/Shutterstock.com; p. 14 Syda Productions/Shutterstock.com; pp. 16–17 Supawadee56/Shutterstock.com; pp. 18–19 everything possible/Shutterstock.com; p. 22 Rawpixel.com/Shutterstock.com; p. 25 Smith Collection/Gado/Archive Photos/Getty Images; p. 28 silverkblackstock/Shutterstock.com; pp. 30, 33, 44 © AP Images; p. 31 Georgejmclittle/Shutterstock.com; p. 37 Saul Loeb/AFP/Getty Images; p. 39 garagestock/Shutterstock.com; p. 42 Sam Kresslein/Shutterstock.com; p. 43 pixinoo/Shutterstock.com; p. 46 Erika Goldring/WME IMG/Getty Images; cover (top) and interior pages background (circuit board) jijomathai/Shutterstock.com; additional interior pages circuit board image gandroni/Shutterstock.com.

Design/Layout: Brian Garvey; Senior Editor: Kathy Kuhtz Campbell; Photo Researcher: Bruce Donnola